Monkey Mystery

Written by Brenda Scott Royce

Illustrated by Joseph Wilkins

JOLLY
FiSH
PRESS
Mendota Heights, Minnesota

Book design by Sarah Taplin
Illustrations by Joseph Wilkins (Beehive Illustration)

Published in the United States by Jolly Fish Press, an imprint of North Star Editions, Inc.

First Edition
First Printing, 2022

This is a work of fiction. Names, characters, places, and incidents are either the product of the author's imagination or are used fictitiously, and any resemblance to actual persons living or dead, business establishments, events, or locales is entirely coincidental.

Library of Congress Cataloging-in-Publication Data (pending)
978-1-63163-620-2 (paperback)
978-1-63163-619-6 (hardcover)

Jolly Fish Press
North Star Editions, Inc.
2297 Waters Drive
Mendota Heights, MN 55120
www.jollyfishpress.com

Printed in the United States of America

TABLE OF CONTENTS

CHAPTER 1

New Volunteers

Katy Nichols couldn't stop smiling. She'd wanted to volunteer at the zoo for as long as she could remember. Now, she was trying on her very own Junior Zoo Volunteer vest. It had the Mountain Bluff Zoo logo on the front. It had "VOLUNTEER" across the back.

"How does it fit?" Luis asked. Luis was the volunteer coordinator. He had a very welcoming smile.

Katy twirled around. "It's perfect," she said. Katy turned to the boy next to her. "How about yours?"

Micah Draper was two years younger and a few inches shorter than Katy. They were best friends.

"I love it," Micah said. "Look, my camera fits inside this pocket."

Micah loved to take pictures. He'd brought his camera along even though Katy didn't think he'd have time for photography. Of course, she'd brought her favorite notebook. Who knows?

She might get a chance to draw some animals.

"Ready for your first assignment?" Luis asked.

"Yes, yes!" the two friends shouted.

Luis led them through the zoo. He pointed out different animals as they walked. At the koala exhibit, they saw a keeper raking leaves.

"Say hello to our koala keeper," Luis said, waving at the woman. "Her name is—"

"Mom!" Katy shouted. "At least, that's what I call her."

The keeper looked up from her task. "Hello, Katy! Hi, Micah!"

"Hi, Corinna," Luis said. "I didn't realize that Katy is your daughter.

We're headed for the monkeys. See you later!"

CHAPTER 2

Meeting Charlie

"Today, you'll be Junior Researchers," Luis said. They had just reached the monkey habitat.

"What's that?" Katy asked.

"Researchers are the eyes and ears of the zoo," Luis answered. "Our keepers are busy caring for all the animals. They rarely have time to sit and observe. If they're worried

about an animal, they call on research
volunteers."

Two monkeys were chasing each
other around the enclosure. A third
lay on a tree branch, hands folded over
his tummy.

"That one looks bigger than the others," Micah said.

"That's Charlie," Luis said. "He's been putting on weight lately. We don't know why. He isn't sick. His diet hasn't changed. Maybe by watching his behavior, you kids can solve the mystery."

Katy scrunched her nose. "We just ... watch?"

Luis nodded. "Watch, listen, and write down anything that might be a clue."

The monkey keeper, Carmen,

came around the side of the monkey enclosure with a bucket of fruits and vegetables. She shouted, "Breakfast time!" The monkeys whooped loudly.

Luis introduced Carmen to the kids and returned to his office. The kids watched Carmen open a chute and toss food inside the exhibit. Charlie grabbed a banana and some broccoli. He began chomping away.

"Well, you know Charlie." Carmen pointed at the two smaller monkeys. "And those two are Willie and Wanda."

"How can you tell them apart?"

Micah asked. "They look exactly the same!"

"Yes, they're twins. But Willie always looks like he's having a bad hair day."

CHAPTER 3

Slow Day

When the monkeys finished eating, Charlie climbed onto a platform. He quickly fell asleep. Willie and Wanda spent most of the morning playing. Later, the siblings groomed each other's fur.

Katy wrote down everything the monkeys did in her notebook. Then she noticed the sign in front of the enclosure. "This says they're capuchin monkeys," she told Micah. "They're found mostly in Central and South America."

Micah didn't answer. Katy turned and saw him sitting on a bench. His were eyes closed.

"Micah!" Katy elbowed him in the ribs. "We're supposed to be watching the monkeys. Junior Researchers are the eyes and ears of the zoo!"

"You be the eyes. I'll be the ears," Micah said, yawning. "Besides, they're not doing anything."

"They are resting," Katy said.

"That's *something*. Anything could be a clue."

Micah's father picked up the kids at the end of their shift. He had just finished his workday at the fire station.

"Hi, Mr. Draper," Katy chirped. "Did you fight any fires today?"

The fireman shook his head. "No, but it was a busy day. We replaced the fire hoses in our trucks. Now there are piles of old hose all over the station, waiting for the garbage collector. They look like mountains of spaghetti!"

As they drove, the kids told Mr. Draper about the monkeys. "They're fun to watch, but so far we haven't found any clues about Charlie's weight gain," Katy said.

Micah yawned. "All we do is write down what the monkeys do. It's boring. I'd rather go to the skate park."

"Today was your first day," his father said. "Give it another chance."

Mr. Draper pulled up to Katy's house. They waved to her grandmother, who was waiting at the door.

As she climbed out of the car, Katy said to Micah, "Maybe tomorrow we'll solve the mystery!"

But Micah wasn't so sure.

CHAPTER 4

The Monkey Maze

When they arrived the next morning, it was feeding time. Once again, the monkeys ate quickly. When his tummy was full, Charlie climbed onto a branch and dozed.

Katy turned to Micah. "Are *you* going to take a nap now too?"

Micah shook his head. "I read about capuchin monkeys last night. They're one of the smartest monkey species."

"Really?" Katy asked. "What else did you learn?"

"In the wild, they travel miles to find their favorite foods. They spend all day swinging and climbing through trees."

Katy looked thoughtful. "At the zoo, they don't have to search for food. And they only have one rope to swing on."

Micah shrugged. "Maybe they're bored."

When Carmen returned, she was carrying a red plastic ball.

"Is that for the monkeys?" Katy asked. Carmen nodded.

"You'd better get a new one," Micah said. "This one has holes in it."

Carmen laughed. "It's a special ball." She unscrewed a cap on the ball and dropped some peanuts through the opening. Then she replaced the cap.

"The monkeys have to move the ball around to get the treats out," Carmen said. "It's a type of enrichment."

"What's enrichment?" Katy asked.

"Something that makes an animal's environment more interesting or challenging. It could be a new object to explore. Or it could be a different way of getting food."

Carmen shook the ball. Hearing the peanuts rattle inside, the monkeys began to jump and whoop. Carmen opened the chute and tossed the ball inside.

"I have to go clean the otter pool," she told the kids. "See you later."

Charlie grabbed the ball in both hands. He shook it forcefully. One by one, the peanuts fell out and were snatched up by the monkeys. When the ball was empty, Charlie tossed it aside.

Micah sighed. "That was fast."

"Not much of a challenge," Katy agreed.

Charlie climbed back onto his favorite branch and closed his eyes.

Katy pulled her notebook and pencil out of her vest pocket. She began to draw. "I have an idea."

"We call it the Monkey Maze," Micah said when they showed Katy's sketch to Carmen. "From the outside it looks like a plain box, but inside there are places to hide treats."

"The ball is too easy for a smart species like capuchins," Katy added. "To get a treat out of this maze, they have to pull the right combination of levers."

Carmen nodded. "It would take them a lot longer to figure out. I'm going to show this sketch to our construction team and see if they can make it. Great job, kids!"

Micah's stomach growled.

"Is the thought of peanuts making you hungry?" Katy asked.

"Actually, I was thinking about spaghetti," Micah said. "And not the kind you eat."

He told Carmen about the piles of fire hose waiting to be tossed in the trash at the station. "I bet the monkeys would love to play with all that fire hose."

Katy's eyes lit up. "They could swing on it, like vines in the jungle!"

"Do you think the firefighters would donate the hose to the zoo?" Carmen asked.

Micah smiled. "I'll ask my Dad!"

CHAPTER 5

Fire Hose Fun

The next Saturday, Micah tugged Katy's arm as they hurried through the zoo. His father had arranged for the station to donate fire hoses to the zoo. Some of them had already been used in the monkey habitat.

"Look!" Katy squealed when she saw Charlie swinging from one hose to another. "I didn't know Charlie could move like that."

The twins bounced on a fire-hose hammock that stretched across one corner of the enclosure.

"The construction crew had fun turning the fire hoses into vines and hammocks," said Carmen. "They also made this." She handed Katy a wooden box. It had knobs and levers, just like in Katy's sketch.

"It's the Monkey Maze!" Micah said. "Does it work?"

"Let's see!" Carmen said. "I put some figs inside the hidden chamber. Figs are Charlie's favorite."

Carmen placed the box inside the habitat. Charlie picked it up and shook it. The figs rattled around inside the box, but none fell out. Now, all three monkeys were curious. They twisted knobs, pulled levers, and slapped the box.

"Maybe it's *too* challenging," Katy worried.

Just then, Charlie pulled the right combination of levers on the box and a fig dropped out. The kids cheered.

When their volunteer shift was over, Carmen thanked them for their help. "Charlie is more active than I've seen him in years! And now he'll need to work harder to get his treats. These

changes are good for his body *and* his brain."

The kids waved goodbye to Carmen and the monkeys. Then Katy turned to Micah. "I wonder what our next volunteer assignment will be?"

THINK ABOUT IT

 Volunteers donate their time to help people, animals, or organizations that they care about. Are there places in your community that need a helping hand?

 Figs are Charlie's favorite treat. He also eats bananas, broccoli, and other fruits and vegetables. Study your favorite animal, and find out what it eats in the wild.

Katy designs the Monkey Maze as enrichment for Charlie. Can you think of an enrichment idea for a dog, cat, or other pet?

ABOUT THE AUTHOR

Brenda Scott Royce is the author of more than twenty books for adults and children. Animals are her favorite subject to write about. She has worked as a chimpanzee keeper at an animal sanctuary and traveled on wildlife expeditions to Africa and South America. In her free time, she helps injured birds as a volunteer with SoCal Parrot Rescue.

ABOUT THE ILLUSTRATOR

Joseph Wilkins is an illustrator living and working in the seaside town of Brighton, England. A graduate of Falmouth College of Arts in Cornwall, Joseph has spent the last fifteen years forging a successful freelance career. When not drawing, he can be found messing around with bicycles or on the beach with his family.

DOGGIE DAYCARE 🐾 IS OPEN FOR BUSINESS!

Join siblings Shawn and Kat Choi as they start their own pet-sitting service out of their San Francisco home. Every dog they meet has its own special personality, sending the kids on fun (and furry) adventures all over the city!

"Shawn and Kat are supported by a diverse cast in which readers of many colors can see themselves reflected. Problem-solvers and dog lovers alike will pounce on this series." —Kirkus Reviews

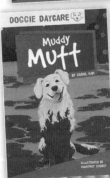